W9-BPL-286

Withdrawn

The Boxcar Children Mysteries

THE ROCK 'N' ROLL MYSTERY

created by
GERTRUDE CHANDLER WARNER

Illustrated by Robert Papp

ALBERT WHITMAN & Company
Morton Grove, Illinois

J
WARNER

The Rock 'n' Roll Mystery
created by Gertrude Chandler Warner;
illustrated by Robert Papp.

ISBN 13: 978-0-8075-7089-0 (hardcover)
ISBN 10: 0-8075-7089-3 (hardcover)
ISBN 13: 978-0-8075-7090-6 (paperback)
ISBN 10: 0-8075-7090-7 (paperback)

Cover art by Robert Papp.

For more information about Albert Whitman & Company,
visit our web site at www.albertwhitman.com.

Contents

THE ROCK 'N' ROLL
MYSTERY

CHAPTER 1

The Greenfield Music Festival

"Benny, are you playing with that *again?*"

Twelve-year-old Jessie Alden stood watching her six-year-old brother. Benny held a ukulele—a very small guitar with four strings. His fingers were struggling to get some sound out of it.

"I can't seem to make it...work," he said, a little frustrated.

He and Jessie were inside a large white tent—one of dozens that had been set up on the fairgrounds at the edge of town. The Greenfield Music Festival drew a huge crowd every year. More than twenty different groups would be performing this year, playing jazz, blues, classical, and rock 'n' roll. The Alden children loved the festival—and this year they'd gotten a chance to be volunteer workers there!

Henry, who at fourteen was the oldest, was helping out in the stage area. Ten-year-old Violet, who was a very good artist, was painting signs. And Jessie and Benny were busy setting up "The Instrument Petting Zoo." It was a special tent run by Mr. Lessenger, who owned a music store in Greenfield, and it was one of the most popular features of the festival. Children could try all types of musical instruments—guitars, violins, drums, horns, and flutes.

Benny shook his head and laughed. "I'm never going to be able to play this!"

"You can if you practice," Mr. Lessenger replied. He was a cheerful older man with white hair and glasses, and he loved helping children discover the joys of music.

"It takes time, Benny," he continued. "Don't be discouraged. The greatest musicians in the world couldn't play a note when they started."

"Really?" Benny asked. That made him feel better.

Most of the instruments were set neatly on their stands, and their cases were stacked in the corner, out of the way. "Looks like you've made some good progress since I was last here," said Mr. Lessenger.

"We're just about finished," Jessie replied. "We just need to make sure everything's in tune."

Mr. Lessenger nodded. "That's great, Jessie. Thanks so much for all your help. And I hope you're having fun playing the instruments. I see Benny on the ukulele over there, but what about you? Have you tried anything?"

"No, not yet," Jessie answered. "But I'm thinking about the piano. I like the sound of pianos very much."

Mr. Lessenger nodded. "That one over there was built over fifty years ago, so it sounds great."

Jessie seemed puzzled by this. "I don't understand. Doesn't it sound worse as it gets older? Doesn't it wear out?"

"Oh, no," Mr. Lessenger replied with a smile. "Many instruments get better with age. They've been played so much that everything gets sort of 'broken in.' I have customers who will pay a lot for older instruments, and custom instruments, too."

"What does 'custom' mean?" Jessie asked as Benny continued plinking and plunking in the background.

"It means it was made just for one person. Many musicians don't buy their instruments in an ordinary store. They order them specially made from scratch."

"Wow, making instruments—that sounds interesting," Jessie said.

"It is," Mr. Lessenger went on. "Custom-made instruments are often more beautiful—and sound much better—than instruments made in factories. Some of the best instruments I've ever had in my store were either very old or custom-made."

Another person joined them in the tent. He was a young man with messy black hair. Mr. Lessenger had introduced him earlier in the morning—his name was Tim, and he worked at Mr. Lessenger's store.

"I'm all done," Tim said. "There's nothing else to unload from the truck, so I'll head back to the store now."

"Okay, good," Mr. Lessenger said. "I'll see you over there in a little while."

Tim turned and left without another word. When the Aldens had first met him, he hadn't seemed very friendly. He just nodded but didn't say hello, and he didn't speak to Jessie or Benny when he carried the instruments from his truck to the tent. Maybe he was just the "quiet type," Jessie thought.

After Tim left, Jessie busied herself tuning the guitars. She had to use something called a "pitch pipe," which had six short silver tubes sticking out of it, three on each side.

When she blew into each tube, a single musical note came out. The six strings on each guitar were supposed to match the six notes made by the pitch pipe. It took Jessie about fifteen minutes to tune all the guitars. Benny's ukulele had already been tuned.

"Okay," Jessie said, "now that that's done, let's take a little break. We'll get some doughnuts, and we'll bring some over to Violet and Henry. They must be hungry, too."

"Oh, boy, doughnuts!" Benny said, jumping off the chair and carefully setting the little ukulele back on its stand. Benny Alden had the biggest appetite of any six-year-old in Greenfield.

They walked together across the big field. It was a bright, sunny day—perfect weather for a festival. At one of the food tents, Jessie bought a bag of powdered doughnuts and four bottles of apple juice. Then she and Benny headed towards the big stage in the middle of the fairground. This was where all the bands would play during the festival.

They'd been watching it go up all morning, and every hour it grew bigger. The stage platform had been built first. Then, two towers of colored lights were put up. After that a row of lights was added across the top, including a huge spotlight. Finally, a giant white curtain was hung as a backdrop.

As they walked toward the stage, Jessie noticed Tim, the young man who worked at Mr. Lessenger's store. He was standing behind a tree—almost as if he was hiding. He was talking to a young woman with a ponytail that was so long it went all the way down her back. Tim had told Mr. Lessenger he was going right back to the store, and yet here he was. Jessie watched as Tim and the girl shook hands. Then Tim looked around, to see if anyone was watching, but he didn't seem to spot Jessie.

That's odd, Jessie thought.

Jessie hurried to catch up with Benny. She didn't say anything to him about Tim. It probably wasn't important, she thought.

* * * *

There were at least twenty people working busily around the stage. One man was fiddling with dozens of knobs and buttons on something called a control board. The Aldens had learned that the control board could change all the sounds during a concert—the high sounds of violins and flutes, and the low sounds of bass guitars and big drums. It could make things louder or softer, and it could also create special effects like echoes. A sign hanging from it said, "Please Do Not Touch."

Another man was testing the lights from a second control board, turning on the green lights first, then the red ones, then the blue ones. There was a certain excitement in the air, too, as if something big was about to happen.

Jessie and Benny found Violet on the other side of the stage, carefully painting a tall wooden sign.

"You look like you could use something to eat and drink," Jessie told her. She was always taking care of her brothers and sister, very much like a mother would.

"Thanks, I sure could." Violet chose one doughnut from the bag and twisted the top off her bottle. She took a long sip of apple juice, then said, "I'm just about done with the sign. How do you think it looks?"

The background had been painted white, and the words "Tonight Only" were in dark Green letters at the top.

"I'm going to add 'the Greenfield Four' and some instruments next," said Violet.

"It's terrific," Jessie said.

"It sure is!" Benny added.

"Thanks," Violet replied. "They're going to hang it up tomorrow night when the band plays."

The Greenfield Four was one of the most popular bands in town. There were two men and two women—all very talented. When the four of them sang together, their voices blended beautifully. They played many different instruments, too. It seemed as though they were good at everything!

The band played in the Greenfield area all the time, often at one of the schools or at a charity event. Alan and Amy Keller were the band's leaders, and they were also married. Karen played piano and guitar, and Dave played drums.

"I'll bet Karen will love the sign," Jessie said to Violet. In addition to being a member of the Greenfield Four, Karen had also been giving Violet guitar lessons for the past few months.

"I hope so," Violet replied. "No one will see it until the end of the festival, since the Greenfield Four will be the last band to play."

"Why's that?" Benny asked.

"Because they're the most popular," Violet said. "It'll be the perfect end to the festival."

"And also," Jessie added, "because the man from the record company will be here then."

"Oh, that's right," Benny said. "I forgot about that. Why is he coming again?"

"He travels all over the country, looking for talented new groups," Jessie told him.

"As soon as he finds them, he has them make albums for him. Then their CDs are sold all over the world."

"So this is the Greenfield Four's big chance to become famous," Violet added.

On the other side of the stage, Henry, the oldest Alden came huffing and puffing as he carried a large coil of black cable over his shoulder. He was followed by a man who was carrying another, larger coil. The man's name was Raymond, and he was a "roadie." He traveled with bands wherever they went, helping to set up all the equipment.

Raymond was small and muscular, with very dark bushy hair and a thick mustache. He was friendly enough, but, like Tim, he seemed kind of quiet. The Aldens also noticed that he was very good at his job.

"Those two have been working so hard," Violet said.

Henry and Raymond came around to the front of the stage. Raymond smiled.

"Thanks for loaning me your brother today. He's been great."

"That's good," Jessie said. "A little hard work never hurt anyone. Right, Henry?"

Henry was still trying to catch his breath. He tried to say something, then just nodded instead. Everyone laughed.

Jessie opened his juice for him and handed it over. Henry drank half of it in one long sip. Then he grabbed a doughnut from the bag and took a big bite.

"I never had any idea how hard it was to build a stage," he said.

"Harder than living in a boxcar?" Jessie asked.

Henry managed to smile. "Well, not as much fun," he replied.

After their parents died, the Aldens had run away from home. They knew that their grandfather was trying to find them, but they had heard that he was mean. They found an abandoned train car—a boxcar in the woods—and cleaned it up so they could live in it. Their grandfather still found them, though, and the children were delighted to learn that he wasn't mean at all. He took them back to his home in Greenfield, and he brought their boxcar along, too! He set it up in the backyard so the children could play in it anytime they wished.

"You do this kind of work every night, don't you Raymond?" Benny asked.

"Just about, Benny," Raymond said. "And it *is* a lot of work. But I'm lucky this time—I have all these great volunteers to help." He patted Henry on the back and said, "Take five minutes, Henry. You've earned it. Then meet me in the back with that cable. We've still got plenty to do."

"Sure," Henry said.

After he was gone, Violet said, "Guess what else I heard?" The others leaned in close. "I heard the TV station is going to come. They're going to show the Greenfield Four's concert on television."

"Wow!" Benny said.

"That's great," Jessie added. "Thousands of people will see them!"

Violet nodded. "That's right. So they've really got to play their very best."

"Boy, I sure hope so," a voice behind them said. The Aldens turned to see Alan Keller from the Greenfield Four. He had sandy blond hair and a deep, powerful voice.

"Hi, Alan," Violet said. "How does everything look?"

"Perfect," Alan replied, admiring the stage. The sparkle in his eyes told the Aldens he couldn't wait to get up there and play.

"Everything is just perfect. And I want to thank you kids again for all the hard work you're doing."

"It's no problem," Henry said. "We're all having fun." The others nodded.

"Well, I'd better get back to the rehearsal studio," Alan said. "There's not much left for us to do now but practice."

"Good luck," Violet told him.

"Thanks." Alan turned and left.

The children spent the rest of their break finishing their juice and doughnuts and watching everyone work on the stage. One man stopped by and said he wished he had a bottle of cold juice just like Henry did, so

Jessie promised to bring him one. Then they watched a woman with a clipboard test the sound system to make sure each speaker worked right. And then there was a tall, thin man who paused to admire Violet's sign. Henry had seen him helping with some of the electrical equipment. He had a beard, glasses, and a black beret.

"Do you like the Greenfield Four, too?" Benny asked him.

"Never heard of them," the man said, though he smiled. The man adjusted his glasses and continued on his way.

Henry checked his watch, then took the last sip of his juice. "Thanks, that was delicious. I have to get back to work now."

"You're welcome," Jessie said. "Come on, Benny, we have to get back, too. Break time's over."

Just as they were about to leave, Alan came around the corner of the stage again. He was closing his cell phone and putting it back into his pocket. He looked pale now, almost sick.

"Are you okay, Alan?" Henry asked.

"I just got a call from Amy," Alan said.

"Is something wrong?" Jessie asked.

Alan looked as though he couldn't believe what he was about to say.

"There sure is—all of our instruments have been stolen!"

CHAPTER 2

Gone!

The children rode their bikes over to
the Greenfield Four's rehearsal studio. It was
a large room with big windows and a high
ceiling. The Aldens had been there several
times during the past week, listening to the
band practice. Everyone had been so excited
about the festival.

But the mood was very different now. Alan
was standing in one corner, speaking quietly
to a Greenfield police officer. Nearby, a

young man was sitting behind his drum kit. Dave was the "funny one" in the group, always quick to make a joke or smile—but he wasn't smiling at the moment. Amy Keller was talking with another police officer, who was taking notes.

Karen looked hurt and confused. She stood on the far side of the room, by a row of empty guitar stands. She was young and pretty, with straggly brown hair and lively green eyes. She stared in disbelief at the empty keyboard racks, the drum kit with no cymbals, and the cables thrown aside carelessly.

When she saw the Aldens, she tried to be cheerful.

"Hi, kids," she said, smiling weakly.

"Karen, we're so sorry," Violet said. "What happened?"

"Someone came in during the night and took most of our equipment."

"Have the police found any clues yet?"

"No," Karen said. "Amy is giving them a list of the items that were stolen."

"It looks like a lot," Violet said.

"It is," Karen told her. "Guitars, basses, horns, keyboards…I don't know how we'll be able to play tomorrow night." As soon as she said this, she looked twice as upset. The concert was supposed to be the band's "big break." Now it looked like it might not happen at all.

"Can't you just borrow some instruments?" Benny asked.

Karen shook her head. "It wouldn't be the same. A lot of our instruments were made just for us."

"You mean they were custom-made?" Jessie asked, remembering what Mr. Lessenger had said before.

"That's right," said Alan. He slumped into a chair next to Karen. "Like my painted guitar. Not only does it look different, it has a special sound, too."

The children had always noticed Alan's guitar at concerts. It was beautiful—the wooden body had been painted with a colorful autumn leaf design.

"We do our best when we play our own instruments." Karen sighed. "And it would take days to program new keyboards." She put her head in her hands. "There's no way we could do that now. We have to get ours back."

"We promise to help," Violet said, trying to make her feel better. "We've solved a few mysteries before."

Karen smiled. "We can use all the help we can get. Time is running out fast."

"Leave it to us!" Benny exclaimed.

After the police were gone, the Aldens went to work. They searched every inch of the big room for clues. Jessie and Benny checked every window, but they were all locked tight. Violet went to each spot where an instrument had been taken, hoping for something like a torn piece of clothing or maybe a footprint on the floor. No such luck. Henry was looking around the door—the only other way into the room aside from the windows—when he noticed a small plastic cover on the wall, next to the light switch.

When he lifted the cover, he found a keypad underneath. The buttons looked like the buttons on a telephone—each one had a number and three tiny letters on it.

"Is this an alarm system?" he asked.

"Yes," Amy replied. She was a tall woman with blond hair. "We had it put in a few years ago."

"It must've been off last night," Henry said. "If it was on and someone broke in, the alarm would've sounded, right?"

The four members of the band looked at each other.

"I figured it had been accidentally left off," Karen said with a shrug.

"Me, too," Dave said. He was twirling a drumstick between two fingers.

"No, I'm sure I turned it on when I left," Alan told them. "That's what I told the police."

Henry looked back at the keypad. "Then how could the thief have broken in without the alarm going off?"

"Good question," Alan replied. He dug

through a cabinet and found the owner's manual to the alarm system. Henry read the manual for a few minutes. He was good at reading instructions, even when they were long. Finally, Henry had it figured out. He tapped a few buttons, and the following words appeared on the little screen—

SYSTEM ACTIVATED 10:33 PM

"Ac-ti-va-ted? What does that mean?" Benny asked. He was still learning to read, and he loved discovering new words.

"Turned on," Jessie told him. "It's when the system was turned on."

"So I did turn it on when I left last night," Alan said.

"It looks that way," Henry said. Then he hit another button, and the screen read—

SYSTEM DEACTIVATED 12:04 AM

"De-ac-ti-va-ted," Benny said. "That must mean the opposite, right?"

"Yes," Jessie told him. "Someone turned the system off just after midnight."

"That's how they got in without setting the alarm off," Violet added.

"They knew the security code," Henry pointed out. "That's the only way they could've done it. They had to know the six-number code."

Jessie looked at the band members. "But who else knows it aside from the four of you? Anyone?"

"Only Raymond," Amy Keller replied. "He was the one who programmed the code. It's '463534.' Very easy for all of us to remember."

Benny made a face. "It doesn't sound easy!"

"It isn't," Amy told him, "until you notice that those numbers can also stand for certain letters on the keypad as well—'GNFLD4.'"

Benny smiled. "Oh, sure, I see now!"

Jessie said, "Do you think...maybe Raymond had something to do with the theft?"

Everyone in the room looked at each other.

"He seems like such a nice person," Violet said. "Didn't you think so, too, Henry?"

"Yeah, very nice," Henry agreed.

"Honestly," Amy Keller said, "I don't know him all that well. He's been with us for a while, but he's so quiet. I have to say I've wondered about him from time to time."

"Well, if someone in the band didn't steal the instruments," Karen said, "then who else could it have been?"

No one had an answer to that.

CHAPTER 3

A Rival?

The Aldens decided to return to the festival grounds to talk with Raymond. They wanted to find out if he had gone back to the rehearsal studio the night before, or if he had given the security code to anyone else.

"Alan seems to think Raymond is totally innocent," Violet said.

"But the others didn't seem as sure," Henry reminded her.

When the Aldens got to the stage, they

quickly realized Raymond was nowhere to be found. Then the children spotted the tall thin man with the beard and the black beret. He was on his knees, working with some wires.

"Excuse me, sir?" Henry asked. The man didn't seem to hear at first, so Henry asked him again.

The man looked up and smiled. "Oh, hi. Sorry I didn't hear you. I get so involved when I'm doing electrical work. Anyway, I'm surprised to see you. I thought you'd left for the day!"

"No, we just had to go over to the Greenfield Four's rehearsal studio."

"So I guess you heard about their instruments being taken," the man said.

"We're going to try to find them!" Benny said.

"That's terrific. Can I help?"

"Actually, you can," Jessie told him. "There was a person here earlier, helping out. His name was Raymond. Have you seen him?"

"He's their roadie, right?" the bearded man asked.

"Yes, that's him!" Violet replied.

The man got to his feet and patted his forehead with a handkerchief. It was very hot, and his eyes were blinking from the bright sunlight.

"I saw him go over there about twenty minutes ago," he said, pointing towards the fairground's main building. "He hasn't come back since," the man added.

"Thanks," Jessie said.

The children had been in the main building before to see a play.

They went through the glass doors at the front, and they found themselves standing in a huge airy lobby. On one wall, there were old posters from past events. The Greenfield Four was on a few of them, the Aldens noticed. Sometimes they were the first band listed. Other times they were second, always beneath another band called "Danny and the Duotones."

"I remember hearing Alan talk about that

group," Violet said. "Remember, the other night, while they were practicing?"

Henry nodded. "He said something about how much Danny would love to play for the man from the record company."

"It seems like they've been rivals for a long time," Violet said.

"What is a 'rival?'" Benny asked.

"A rival is someone who wants the same thing that you do," Jessie told her brother.

At that moment, they heard a familiar voice—it was Raymond, in a nearby hallway, talking to someone.

The Aldens went over there slowly, and when they peered around the corner they saw him—on a pay phone.

"We shouldn't be listening to his private conversation," Jessie said.

Henry agreed. "Let's wait for him outside."

But as they turned to go, they couldn't help overhearing Raymond say, "That's right, it looks like the Greenfield Four will lose their big chance now."

Jessie held her breath. Who was Raymond talking to?

"They don't have anything to play with," Raymond went on. "No guitars, no keyboards, nothing. They lost it all. Looks like you're the one who got lucky. Will you be ready to go on in their place if they can't get their act back together?" Raymond asked. "Yeah? Okay, good. Then I'll be over to give you a hand in a few minutes. Bye."

The children hurried back outside before Raymond saw them. They watched from behind some bushes as Raymond hopped onto his bike and rode off.

"Was he talking to someone from another band?" Jessie wondered.

"Maybe we should get on our own bikes and see where he's going," Violet suggested.

Henry nodded. "Good idea, Violet," he replied. "Let's go."

* * * *

The Aldens were careful to follow Raymond from a safe distance—they didn't want to risk having him notice them. At one point, as they passed through the center of town, he actually stopped, turned around, and waved. But he wasn't waving at them. It was someone passing by in a car. The Aldens felt very relieved when they saw the driver wave back.

Raymond cut through town and went into one of Greenfield's quieter areas, with lots of large, beautiful homes. He turned onto Knickerbocker Road. When the Aldens reached the corner, they saw that he had disappeared!

"Where'd he go?" Violet wondered, looking in every direction.

Knickerbocker Road had tall, handsome oak trees on either side. Neighborhood children were playing on the sidewalks, and cars were parked here and there—but there was no sign of Raymond.

"I'm sure he went down this street," Henry said, scratching his head. "Or did I imagine it?"

"Well, if you did," Jessie told him, "then we all did!"

"Okay," Henry replied, "then let's keep going and see what happens. Keep your eyes and ears open."

They cycled on, watching and listening very carefully. But there was no sign of Raymond. Did he really just disappear?

"Maybe he did know we were following him and hid somewhere," Jessie suggested. "Behind a bush or a car or something."

"I was thinking the same thing," Henry said. "If he's sneaky enough to steal all those instruments without anyone knowing, then he's probably sneaky enough to—"

Henry's bicycle suddenly squealed to a stop. The other three Aldens stopped right behind him. He had spotted a house with its garage door up.

"Look!" Henry said.

Raymond's bicycle was parked in the driveway. But what really caught the Aldens' attention was the open garage. Inside, the garage looked like a rehearsal studio. There was a drum kit, several keyboards, one big piano, a collection of horns, a few guitars—

including one that had a very unusual design. Violet gasped when she saw that the body was painted with bright autumn leaves.

"It's Alan's guitar!" she whispered in shock.

CHAPTER 4

One of a Kind?

The Aldens stood in the driveway and stared at the open garage.

"Are you sure this is one of the stolen guitars?" Henry asked Violet. Violet nodded. The children knew Violet had a good eye for details.

"It has to be Alan's guitar," Jessie put in. "He said it was custom-made."

"And now it's over there!" Benny said.

"But who lives here?" Jessie wondered—

"Whose house is this?"

"I don't know," Henry said, "but I'll bet it's the same person Raymond was talking to on the phone before. Let's wait and see if someone comes out." Henry got off his bicycle and set it against a nearby tree. The other Aldens did the same.

They didn't have to wait long. A door inside the garage opened, and a tall figure stepped out from inside the house.

"Oh, my!" Violet said. "That's—"

"Danny Duellman!" Jessie finished. "I remember seeing his face on some of those posters!"

Henry was nodding slowly. "Of course—it all makes perfect sense. If the Greenfield Four couldn't play tomorrow night, then Danny and the Duotones would take their place."

"And his band would get to play in front of the man from the record company!" Jessie added.

"So Danny Duellman robbed the Greenfield Four?" Violet asked, stunned.

Danny Duellman didn't notice the Aldens standing out on the sidewalk. He went over to Alan's guitar, lifted it gently off its stand, and set it carefully into a case. He then closed the case and locked it. *Was he trying to hide it?* Jessie wondered.

"Excuse me," Henry said.

Danny turned quickly; he wasn't expecting anyone to be there.

"We're friends of the Greenfield Four," Jessie said, taking a deep breath, "and we'd like to ask you a question about that guitar." At that moment, the door leading into the house opened again, and the children looked up. *Is Raymond here?* Jessie thought. But it wasn't Raymond. It was Alan Keller.

What was the leader of the Greenfield Four doing here?

Alan seemed as surprised as they were.

"Why, it's the Aldens," he said. "Have you met my friend Danny Duellman?"

The Aldens couldn't believe their ears—Danny was Alan's friend?

Danny walked over to them with his hand

out. "It's very nice to meet all of you. I'm the lead singer for Danny and the Duotones." Then he made sure to add, "Maybe you've heard of us?"

Still shocked, Jessie managed to say, "Uh, sure. We've heard of you."

"Well, that's good news," Danny went on. "And what were you about to ask me?"

"That guitar you just put away," Jessie began, suddenly feeling much less certain of the situation. "Isn't that...Alan, isn't that your guitar?"

Violet added, "We thought we saw it at the rehearsal studio yesterday. You were playing it."

"Playing it?" Alan said. "No, I wasn't play—oh, wait a minute." He could see that the Aldens needed an explanation. "That guitar looks like one of a kind," he began, and the children nodded. "But really, there are *two*. I have one, and Danny has the other. We had them both painted by an artist friend a few years ago."

"Ohhhh," the Aldens said altogether.

"There are no others like them in the world," Danny added.

"But aren't you two…rivals?" Jessie asked.

"Sure," Alan said. "Rivals, but not enemies. Actually, the fact that we're both trying to get the same things is what makes us so good. It makes us try harder."

"That's right," Danny continued. "I always try to be better than Alan, and he tries to be better than me. We've been doing this for years. See?" He pointed to some framed pictures that were hanging on the wall. They were more old flyers from when both bands played years ago. The children also couldn't help noticing that some of them said "The Greenfield Five" and even "The Greenfield Six."

"You used to have more people in your group?" Jessie asked Alan.

"Yes. We've had many people come and go," Alan replied. "Same with Danny."

Danny sighed. "It's hard to find good musicians who all play well together, but sooner or later you do. That's why Alan's band is going to become world-famous before mine. He's found that magical mix of people. I'm still waiting for that to happen."

Alan smiled. "One day it'll happen, Danny. I promise. And I can't thank you enough for your help." He turned to the Aldens. "Danny is loaning me this guitar," he explained. "We hope the Greenfield Four can still play tomorrow night, if we borrow enough instruments."

"What if you can't?" asked Benny.

"Then my band will play in their place," Danny said. "But I'd hate for that to happen. Everyone at the festival wants to see the Greenfield Four tomorrow." He looked thoughtful. "I guess it would be a lucky break if I played. But if the Duotones ever make it big, it shouldn't be just because we're lucky. It ought to be because we're talented and work hard, just like Alan and his band."

The Aldens could see that Danny was a good friend to Alan.

Danny went on. "Today we're calling every musician in town to see if they can help out the Greenfield Four. Raymond, our roadie, is on the phone right now. He works for the Duotones, the Greenfield Four, and other bands, so he knows plenty of people."

The children exchanged looks with each other. Now they knew why Raymond had come here—he worked for Danny's band, too. Just then, Raymond came into the garage holding a cordless phone.

"I just heard a band over in Silver City has a spare bass guitar," he told Danny and Alan. "I'll call them next."

"Can we help?" Jessie asked.

"I heard you're already helping out," Raymond said. "Alan told me you're looking for clues about the thief."

"We sure are!" said Benny.

"We wanted to ask you about the security alarm at the rehearsal studio, actually," said Henry. "Does anyone else besides you and the band have the code number?"

"No," Raymond replied. "I know for a fact that only the five of us have the code. There was an old code, but I changed it to

463534—GNFLD4—just to be safe. I've been racking my brain trying to figure out how someone got in."

"So have we," said Henry. Jessie, Violet, and Benny nodded.

CHAPTER 5

A Clue and a Keyboard

"I'm glad Raymond isn't the thief," said Violet. "Or Danny Duellman."

Jessie agreed. "And it's nice that they're both helping out the Greenfield Four."

The girls were at the rehearsal studio unpacking bags of sandwiches. Henry was opening up the soda, and Benny was counting napkins. The children didn't have any new clues, but they still wanted to be helpful, so they decided to bring lunch to the band.

"Still, we're right back where we started with this mystery," Henry said.

"Don't feel bad," Karen said. She was sitting nearby, with a guitar on her lap. She'd borrowed it from a friend and was trying to tune it. "You tried your best. The police aren't having any luck, either."

Dave, the drummer, was also there. "We'll have to do the best we can with all this borrowed stuff," Dave grumbled. "I'm glad I could find another set of cymbals, but I think I could get a better sound out of a bunch of garbage-can lids." He tapped them a few times with a drumstick and frowned.

Karen said, "He's right—we'll just have to work with what we've got and hope everything sounds okay." She strummed the borrowed guitar again and sighed. "This doesn't sound right. I need to go to Lessenger's to buy some new strings."

When Karen mentioned the music store, Jessie sat up straight in her chair.

"I just remembered! This morning, after Benny and I helped Mr. Lessenger set up the

Instrument Petting Zoo, I noticed something," she said. "I'm not sure if it's a clue or not, but it was certainly odd. You know that boy Tim who works there?"

"He has dark messy hair, right?" Henry asked. "Sort of quiet?"

"That's him!" said Benny.

"Well, after we finished setting up the tent, Tim told Mr. Lessenger he was going right back to the store," Jessie went on. "But he didn't do that." She told the others how she had spotted him talking to a girl with a long ponytail at the festival grounds.

"Maybe that was his girlfriend," Violet suggested.

"I don't think so," said Jessie. "They shook hands, as if they didn't know each other. And then he kept looking around, as if he wanted to make sure no one was watching."

"They could have been talking about anything," Henry pointed out.

"I suppose," Jessie said. "But...I don't know. I just have a feeling that he could be involved somehow. Just a hunch."

"Why don't we go to Lessenger's Music Store and pick up Karen's guitar strings?" said Henry. "Maybe Tim will be there."

"Good idea," said Violet.

"I second that," said Karen, fishing money out of her purse to pay for the guitar strings. She handed the bills to Jessie. "Good luck," she said.

* * * *

Lessenger's was an exciting place if you loved music. One room had nothing but drums and cymbals, another had brass horns like trumpets and trombones. There was a room only for guitars, and another for recording equipment. And there was always music playing in the store—not just from the speakers in the ceiling, but from shoppers trying out instruments.

The children didn't see Tim or Mr. Lessenger when they first walked in, but it didn't take long to find them. They heard Mr. Lessenger's voice coming from the guitar room—and they were surprised at how angry he sounded.

"If I've told you once, I've told you a hundred times: do not buy a used instrument unless I see it first!"

The Aldens went over to the doorway. Behind the counter, Mr. Lessenger stood and scolded Tim.

"I know," Tim said sheepishly, "and I'm sorry. It just seemed like such a good deal."

"That's exactly why you should have been suspicious!" Mr. Lessenger replied. "A deal that seems too good to be true usually is! Now the store is out three hundred dollars!" he went on. "If this happens again, Tim..." He sighed. "Well, let's just hope it doesn't, okay?"

"Yes, sir," Tim answered.

Mr. Lessenger disappeared into his office, closing the door with a slam.

Tim stood there for a moment, looking upset. Then he spotted the Aldens and tried his best to put on a smile.

"Hi, can I help you with something?"

The Aldens weren't sure what to do or say, either. That had been such a nasty scene!

Jessie finally said, "Uh, you're Tim, aren't you?"

"Yeah, Tim the fool. That's my full name. Do I know you?"

"Don't you remember us from the festival this morning?" Jessie asked. "You helped us set up the Instrument Petting Zoo."

"Oh, sure, I remember. What's up? Did I do something wrong over there, too?"

"Oh," Jessie said quickly. "We were just wondering—we noticed you were talking to a girl. She had a ponytail, very long."

Tim gave out a little laugh. "Yeah, I bought a used keyboard from her. That's why I just got yelled at."

"Why would you get in trouble for that?" Henry asked. "You sell used instruments here, don't you?"

"Yes," Tim replied, "but this one was a little different—it was stolen."

"Stolen!" Jessie said. "How do you know?"

"Here, I'll show you," Tim said. He disappeared into a back room and returned a moment later with the keyboard in his arms.

It was long, black, and very heavy with knobs and buttons above the keys.

"See this?" Tim said. He pointed to a spot at the back. Henry carefully turned the keyboard around. And there, right by the button that turned it on and off, was a name scratched into the metal—"Amy Keller."

"Oh my goodness!" Violet said. "This belongs to the Greenfield Four! It's one of the missing instruments!"

"Yeah," Tim said, nodding and looking very unhappy. "I didn't know their stuff had been stolen until Mr. Lessenger told me."

"And you bought it from that girl?" Jessie asked. "The one with the long ponytail?"

"That's right," Tim said. "She wanted to know if I was interested in buying a great keyboard really cheap."

"If it seemed like such a good deal, then why didn't you tell Mr. Lessenger about it first?" Henry asked.

Tim paused before speaking. He suddenly seemed uneasy.

"Because," he said, "I had my own reasons

for buying it from her, too. She was wearing a Glenwood Studios shirt, and she said she worked there. My buddies and I have a band, but we can't afford to go there and record our music. So she and I made a little deal—I would buy the keyboard from her, and she would let us use the studio for free for a few weeks when no one else was in there." He shook his head. "Like I said, it seemed like such a great deal. We could've sold this for seven or eight hundred dollars. I thought Mr. Lessenger would be thrilled."

"I wonder if this girl has any of the other stolen instruments," Henry said.

"Do you think she's the one who stole the instruments in the first place?" Jessie wondered.

Tim spoke up. "I doubt it. I don't know her very well, but she's come into the store before. Her name is Zoey."

"If the thief sold the instruments to a total stranger, then no one would know they were stolen to begin with," Henry pointed out. "It doesn't sound like Zoey is the thief."

Tim agreed. "I bet she'd be just as surprised as I was to find out the keyboard was stolen." He added, "My boss is calling the police right now to tell them one of the stolen instruments turned up. I'm sure they'll want to talk to her soon."

So do we, thought Jessie.

CHAPTER 6

The Girl with the Ponytail

"Jessie, tell us again why you think we should talk to Zoey," Henry said, as he and Violet and Benny followed their sister out of the public library. Jessie had insisted they look up the address of Glenwood Studios in the local business directory.

"Because the studio is just two blocks away from here," she said. "And I'm sure the police will get to the bottom of all this soon enough, but…"

"But what?" said Violet.

"But I keep getting this feeling that the person who stole all these instruments is right under our noses somehow," Jessie said.

"I know what you mean," said Henry.

"Me too," Violet added.

"Me three," said Benny.

"And what's more," Jessie went on, "I don't think this is just a case of someone stealing things to make money. Someone is trying to really hurt the Greenfield Four and ruin their show at the festival tomorrow."

"I wish we knew why," said Violet.

"Exactly," said Jessie. "And what if we're close to finding out?"

"Let's talk to Zoey!" Benny exclaimed.

Glenwood Studios was a small building with a tiny parking lot next to it. Inside, the lobby was decorated with framed photos of musicians who had recorded here. A young man was sitting at the front desk, wearing a GLENWOOD STUDIOS T-shirt.

"Is Zoey here?" she asked the young man.

"Studio A," he said, pointing to the right.

As the children walked down the hallway, they could hear a vacuum cleaner in one of the recording rooms. They peered in and found the girl with the long ponytail there. "That must be Zoey," Jessie said.

Zoey didn't notice them at first, and continued to vacuum the carpet as well as the walls, which were covered with a funny foam material.

"Why are the walls soft?" Benny asked.

"They help absorb noise," replied Henry. "It helps the music sound better while it's being recorded."

"THEN WHY IS THAT VACUUM SO LOUD?" Benny shouted.

Just then, Zoey noticed the children and shut off the vacuum cleaner.

At first she seemed surprised, then she smiled and said, "Oh, hi. Do you have an appointment?"

"No," Jessie said. "Actually, we wanted to talk to you."

"To me?"

"Yes. Did you sell a used keyboard to Tim,

the boy who works at Lessenger's music store, earlier today?"

Suddenly Zoey seemed worried. "Yes, I did," she said. "Is there a problem with it?"

"Well…" Jessie said. She and Henry told Zoey how the Greenfield Four's rehearsal studio had been robbed. "They're our friends," Jessie said.

"Oh, no!" Zoey moaned, rolling her eyes. "I knew it!"

"Knew what?" Violet asked.

"I knew there had to be a catch!" she said. "Here, I'll show you."

The children followed her outside to the parking lot where her small red car was parked. She opened the trunk, and inside was a second keyboard. The Aldens recognized it immediately. They looked near the on/off switch and found the name "Amy Keller" again, scratched into the metal.

"I bought this keyboard this morning, along with the other one that I sold to Tim. I didn't need two, so I figured I'd sell one. I made enough money selling the first one to pay for both of them, so I sort of got this one for free." She sighed. "Or so I thought. I guess I'll have to give the money back to Lessenger's and give both keyboards to the Greenfield Four."

"Who sold the keyboards to you?" Jessie asked.

"I didn't get his name," Zoey said, taking a deep breath, "but here's what happened. I pulled into the parking lot this morning, and a van pulled in behind me. A man got out and started talking to me. I normally don't talk to strangers, but he seemed to know Glenn, my boss, so I figured he was okay. Anyway, he wanted to know if I wanted to buy some instruments—cheap. He opened the back of the van, and there were the two keyboards."

"Were there any other instruments inside?" Henry asked.

"Yes," Zoey said, "some guitars and other things. He said he was giving up music and moving out west, and he wanted to sell his equipment to raise money for the trip. I took the keyboards inside, plugged them in, and they both worked great. So I gave him the money, and off he went."

"What did he look like?" Jessie asked.

"He was tall and thin. He had very dark hair, and a beard and mustache. He was also wearing glasses."

"Hmm," Henry said. "That could be a lot of people. Anything else?"

"Well, the van he was driving was white," Zoey replied. "And it had a big blue stripe running across the sides. It was all beat-up, too. Kind of old."

Jessie was carefully writing down Zoey's description on a spare page in Violet's sketchbook. *Beard and mustache, glasses, white van*—it wasn't much to go on. Was it someone the children had seen working at the festival? Jessie tried to remember. *Maybe this person isn't right under our noses after all*, she thought. Was there anything else she could ask Zoey?

"What was the man wearing?" she asked.

"Oh, my goodness, I almost forgot!" said

Zoey. "He was wearing a beret. One of those funny little hats that artists wear."

Jessie nodded excitedly and looked at Henry. They were both sure they'd seen someone wearing a beret recently. But who?

"I'm glad you asked me," Zoey went on. "I guess I don't tend to imagine hats on people, because so few people wear them. But I did notice the beret. And I'm definitely going to remember it when I call the police and tell them what I know. In fact, I'd better do that now." She reached for her cell phone.

"That's a good idea," Henry said. "And thank you for talking to us, too."

Zoey waved good-bye to the children from the parking lot as they walked back to the street.

"I know we saw a man wearing a beret sometime today," said Violet. "Was it at the festival?"

"I think so," said Jessie. "But we saw a lot of people there."

"Whoever the man in the beret is," said Henry, "he certainly didn't steal any of those instruments for the money."

Jessie agreed. "He sold those keyboards for nearly nothing. He must have some other motive, which is—"

"—to ruin things for the Greenfield Four," Violet finished.

Benny had been quiet all this time.

"What does a beret look like?" he asked finally. "Because that man we talked to this morning, the one with the beard—he had something funny on his head."

The children stopped in their tracks.

"You mean, the man who was working around the stage?" Violet asked. She remembered how he'd stopped to admire the sign she'd painted.

"And then later we asked him if he'd seen Raymond," Jessie said, remembering.

"He was friendly," Henry noted. "But you know what's odd? First he said he didn't know who the Greenfield Four were. But then when we talked to him again, he knew Raymond was their roadie."

"That *is* strange," Jessie said. "Very

strange. We ought to tell the band that this man might be the thief. We can tell the police, too! If only..." her voice trailed off. "If only we knew his name."

The other children nodded sadly. There wasn't much they could do without knowing the man's name.

"Maybe the Greenfield Four will know who he is," Violet said, hopeful. "We can describe him."

"That's true," said Henry.

"Speaking of the Greenfield Four," Benny thought of something. "What happened to their poster?"

He pointed to a nearby phone pole. The children could see that a poster had been torn off recently—only a few scraps at the corners remained. Even from the torn pieces they could tell it had been a poster for the Greenfield Four's show at the festival. The children had helped design the poster, and they could recognize Violet's artwork in the corners.

"Look! There's another one," Benny said

as he spotted a second torn poster on the fence across the street. As the children continued down the street, they could see that nearly all the Greenfield Four's posters had been torn down.

"What happened to them?" Violet wondered. "Did the band take them down because they aren't going to be playing?"

"I hope not," Jessie replied. "I hope they're not giving up yet."

"Maybe someone else did it," Henry suggested. He was about to say something else as they turned the corner. Just then, though, they saw a van pull to the side of the road half a block ahead of them. Then a hand reached out, grabbed one of the posters from a telephone pole, and ripped it off. After that the driver hit the gas, and with screeching tires, the van disappeared.

"Did you see that?" Henry said.

"I sure did," Jessie answered. "And did you see what the van looked like?"

"It was white," Benny said, "with a blue stripe."

"Just like the one Zoey told us about!" Violet said.

"That's right," Henry nodded. "I think that was our thief."

CHAPTER 7

The Man with the Van

When the children returned to the Greenfield Four's rehearsal studio, they told the band everything they'd found out.

"I'm glad my keyboards turned up," said Amy. "But who is this man in the beret?"

The other members of the band shrugged. "We have no idea," Karen said. "I suppose we'll have to let the police figure it out from here."

Later that afternoon the children went to

the Greenfield Diner to meet Grandfather for dinner.

"When we told the band about the man with the beard and the beret, they said they had no idea who he was," Jessie said.

"And aside from the keyboards," Violet added, "everything else is still missing."

"We told the police what he looked like," Henry said. "Maybe that will help."

"Perhaps it will," Grandfather said.

The Aldens ate quietly for a few minutes. It was a busy night at the diner, filled with good smells and the sound of people talking. Whenever the Aldens came here, they always sat in the same place—a large booth by the front. It was quiet and cozy. One of the things Benny liked about it was that it was right by a big window. He could see everything that was happening on Greenfield's main street.

He got up on his knees to look outside. He was chewing on another chicken finger when he noticed a van parked across the street. He stopped chewing. He remembered what

Zoey had said about the van the thief was driving.

"Look!" Benny said. "A van! A white one with a blue stripe!"

Everyone, including Grandfather, got up to see.

"Oh my goodness, Benny's right!" Violet said. "That's exactly like the one we saw!"

"Did you see anyone get in or out of it, Benny?" Henry asked.

"No, no one," Benny said.

Grandfather paid the check quickly, and soon the Aldens headed outside to look over the van.

Benny was right—it looked just like the one they saw earlier. It was white, with a thick blue stripe down each side, and it was dirty, dented, and rusty.

"I'm going to take a look in the window," Henry said. Carefully, he walked around to the back window and peered inside. He was hoping to see the Greenfield Four's stolen instruments.

Instead, the back of the van was filled with

wood and tools—saws, hammers, drills, and jars full of nails and screws.

"What's in there?" Violet asked. "Any guitars?"

"No," Henry replied, disappointed.

"Can I help you?" said a voice from behind them.

The Aldens turned to find a man about Grandfather's age standing on the sidewalk. He was dressed in jeans, a plaid flannel shirt, and leather work boots. His clothes were covered sawdust. The children could tell that the man was a carpenter. He looked at them with a friendly but puzzled expression.

Grandfather stepped forward and shook the man's hand and introduced his the children.

"I'm sorry, sir," Jessie said, "we didn't mean to snoop."

"We were looking for some musical instruments," Violet added.

The carpenter smiled. "Ah, well, I used to play a harmonica pretty well when I was your age, but that's about it."

"No, sir, we were looking for some stolen instruments," Henry replied. He and the other children explained everything that had happened so far.

"And the thief was driving a van exactly like this one," said Jessie. "Just our luck that there are two of them."

"Oh, there are many vans like this around here," the carpenter said. "It's a rental."

"A rental?" Benny asked. "What's that?"

"It means I'm borrowing it," the carpenter replied. "My own van is being fixed right now, so I'm renting this one from a place called Drive-It-Yourself. They have lots of vans just like this."

Jessie's eyes widened. "The thief must have rented a van from the same place!"

The others were nodding. They all thought the same thing.

CHAPTER 8

Mr. Fred Parker of Greenfield

The next morning was bright and beautiful, perfect for the Greenfield Music Festival. As Grandfather drove past the fairgrounds, the Aldens could see the crowds beginning to gather. They spotted a truck from the television station in the parking lot. Even from the back seat of the car, the children could sense the excitement in the air at the Greenfield Music Festival.

"We'll be there soon," Jessie reminded the others.

"But first we have to go to the van rental place to help the police, right?" asked Benny.

"Right," said Grandfather. "I called my good friend Officer Weiss last night, and he's meeting us there. He thinks you've discovered an important clue about the thief's van. Now the next step is to find out more about the person who rented the van."

"Who just might be the same man we talked to at the festival yesterday morning," Henry added. "And maybe someone who works at the Drive-It-Yourself counter will remember him, too."

The Drive-It-Yourself Car Rental Agency was a tiny place on a quiet road. The parking lot was filled with cars, trucks, and vans— and they were all white with blue stripes.

The children went inside. The office was brightly lit and very neat. And, just like the cars and trucks outside, the walls had been painted white, with a large blue stripe. It ran around the entire room.

Grandfather waved to Officer Weiss, who was standing at the front counter. He was speaking to a woman there. The gold name tag on her shirt said that her name was Barbara. She looked up and smiled at the children.

"Don't tell me one of you wants to rent a truck!" she said, chuckling.

The children laughed. "No, ma'am," Henry replied. "We're trying to catch the person who stole the Greenfield Four's instruments."

"Oh, yes. Officer Weiss just told me what happened. How awful," she said. "And I certainly do remember renting a van to a man with a beard and a black beret."

"Do you remember anything else about him?" Jessie asked.

"Let's see…I remember that he seemed very nice," Barbara said. "I also remember that he was having trouble with his eyes."

"What do you mean?" Henry asked.

"He kept blinking and rubbing them," Barbara told him. "When I asked if he was okay, he said it was just allergies. But he took his glasses off before filling out the rental form, which I thought was strange. Most people put their glasses on when they fill out forms."

"I remember him blinking a lot, too." Violet said. The others nodded. "But what kind of a clue is that?" she added.

"It doesn't sound like a very good one," Henry whispered.

Barbara had turned back to Officer Weiss. "Here's the form he filled out to rent the truck" she said. "It says his name is Mr. Fred Parker."

"Does it say where he lives?" the police officer asked.

"Right here in Greenfield," Barbara told him. "On Carteret Street."

Jessie spoke up just then. "Excuse me, but that can't be right," she told Officer Weiss. "There's nothing on Carteret Street but the shopping mall."

"Hmm," said Officer Weiss. "That's right. I'll have to check, but I think Mr. Parker may have given us a fake address." He shook his head. "It figures."

"Can't you catch him when he brings the van back?" Benny asked.

Barbara shook her head. "We have many different offices all over the country. If someone rents a car or a truck here in the Greenfield office, they can return anywhere else. Even somewhere as far away as California."

"He could be anywhere by now," the police officer said with a frown. "We'll alert other police departments. One way or another, we'll track him down."

"Do you think you'll catch him before the Greenfield Four play tonight?" Benny asked, hopefully. "So that they can get their instruments back?"

"We'll try. Sometimes we're able to catch a thief right away," Officer Weiss said. But the children could tell that even he didn't think the thief would be caught in time.

* * * *

Later, the Aldens sat in their sunny

kitchen, but their moods were not sunny. They had tried their best to find the person who had stolen the Greenfield Four's instruments, and now they were at a dead end. The phone book was open on the table. Henry flipped through the pages.

"Nope," he said, "no Fred Parker. I'm sure the man who rented the van made up everything that he put on that form."

Grandfather came in and sat down. "That's what Officer Weiss told me. I just got off the phone with him." He took off his reading glasses and sighed. "I think you've done your best. Now we'll all have to wait until the police find this thief."

Jessie looked at Grandfather's glasses on the table. They made her think of something. "Benny, remember when you tried on Grandfather's glasses last month?"

"Yes," Benny said. "I thought they would make me see better. But they made me see worse! And they felt strange. They made my eyes go like this!" He blinked several times. Everyone laughed.

"That's very funny," said Henry, "but what does that have to do with the mystery?"

"I think it's another clue," Jessie replied. "Remember what the woman at Drive-It-Yourself told us? She said the man with the beret kept rubbing his eyes. And he was blinking a lot when he was talking to us at the festival yesterday, but we thought it was because of the bright sun."

"But maybe it's because he doesn't really wear glasses!" Violet said. "So his eyes were bothered by the pair he had on."

"Those glasses must have been part of a disguise," Henry said. "It makes sense—if he didn't want anyone to know his real name or address, he probably wouldn't want anyone to know what he really looked like, either."

"I think you're right," Grandfather said.

"Now if only we knew what he really looked like," said Jessie. "But of course, we don't."

The Aldens couldn't remember the last time they had a mystery they couldn't solve.

* * * *

The mood in the Greenfield Four's rehearsal studio wasn't much better. The Aldens had stopped by to listen to the band's last rehearsal before their big performance at the festival. The band had borrowed enough instruments to play their songs, but the sound still wasn't quite the same.

"Let's just try to do the best we can tonight," Amy told the others after they finished the last song. "That's what's really important."

Jessie nodded and turned to smile at her sister and brothers. Even though they hadn't found the thief, they were doing the best that they could, too. Henry, Violet, and Benny smiled back.

The band took a break—Dave got up to stretch his legs, and Amy and Alan sat at the folding table to go over their sheet music. Karen went to the piano and played around with a new song the band had written. And the Aldens began to look through Jessie's notebook to make sure there weren't any clues they had missed.

Jessie went over the list of everyone they had talked to. "Raymond the roadie, Danny Duellman, Tim from the music store, Zoey from the studio, the carpenter, and Barbara at Drive-It-Yourself. I think they've told us everything they know," she said.

"Yes," Henry said. "Wait, what's this?" He pointed to two numbers Jessie had written down: 463534 and 463535. "I remember that first number—that's the security code for the studio. But what about the second number?"

"That's the old code," Jessie said. "The one that Raymond said he'd changed to 463534—GRNFLD4. Wow, I forgot I'd asked him for the old number, too. It didn't seem very important at the time."

Henry looked thoughtful. "Hmm. If the code they're using now spells out 'GRN-FLD4,' then the old code spells out—"

"'GRNFLD5!'" Benny finished.

"For the Greenfield Five," said Jessie. "Their old band name."

"Maybe Raymond changed the code to go with the new name," Henry said. But he wondered—*was that the only reason?*

Violet had noticed a colorful binder on top of the piano. It said "Greenfield Four Photo Album" on the cover.

"Hey, that's neat. Can I take a look?" Violet asked Karen.

Inside were dozens of photographs, newspaper clippings, and old flyers, all carefully organized and set behind plastic sheets. Violet could follow the history of the band page by page.

When she was near the middle of the book, she stopped with a gasp. "Oh my goodness!" she said. The children gathered around.

Violet pointed to one of the flyers. *The Greenfield Five in Concert*, it read. There was a photograph of the band below the headline. The children knew all of the faces in the photo—except one.

"Look at this person right here!" Violet said, pointing to the stranger.

"What about him?" Henry asked.

"Doesn't he look familiar?"

"No," Jessie replied, shaking her head. "Not really."

Violet picked up a pencil and started scribbling on the man's face. The others couldn't really see what she was doing. Then she pulled her hand out of the way. She had added a beard, a mustache, a pair of glasses, and a beret.

"I can't believe it," Jessie whispered. "That's the man we saw yesterday. Now we know what he really looks like!"

"And now we know who he is," said Henry. "He used to be in the band!"

CHAPTER 9

The Angry Man

The children showed the Greenfield Four the flyer with Violet's drawing. One by one, Alan, Amy, Karen, and Dave passed it around. They didn't speak for a moment.

Finally, Alan Keller said, "His name is Jon Emmott. And yes, I think he's the thief." The other band members nodded. "Jon was part of the group for about a year," Alan went on. "He played a few different instruments and could sing pretty well. He wasn't bad."

"But…" Amy said, and her frown told the Aldens that she didn't care much for Emmott. "He was a tough person to deal with every day."

"How so?" Jessie asked.

"He had a lot of talent," Karen replied, "but not as much as he thought he did. He acted as if he was the greatest musician and singer in the world."

"Is that why he left?" Violet asked.

"No," Alan said. "He left because we had a big argument one day about what kind of music we should play."

"We had one idea," Amy continued, "and he had another. So he decided to leave."

"He was pretty nasty about it, too," Karen said. "I remember that last day very well. He was telling us how he was going to put his own band together, and it would be so much better than ours."

The Aldens shook their heads. "Sounds like a pretty angry person," Henry said.

"Yes," Alan said. "Jon could also be very

jealous. When he left, he moved out to California. He started his own band, just like he said he would. But they didn't do too well. The last I heard, they broke up, and he had to go back to his old job as an electrician. At the same time, our band was doing really well."

"He must have heard about the man from the record company coming to the festival, and he decided to come back and try to ruin the show," Amy said. "But we're not about to let it get ruined."

"That's right," Karen and Alan added. The children could see that the band was determined to succeed.

Just then the door to the rehearsal studio opened and Raymond came in.

"It's time to get ready for the show," he told the band. Then he turned and noticed the Aldens. "Did you manage to find the thief?" he asked.

The children showed Raymond the scrapbook and the picture of Jon Emmott. He couldn't believe his eyes.

"I've seen him before!" he said.

"So have we," Henry said. "We saw him helping out at the festival. Violet recognized him through his disguise. She drew the beard, glasses, and the beret."

"But now we don't know where he is," Jessie said.

"He could be anywhere!" Benny added.

"That's true," Raymond said. Just then, the children noticed he had a wry smile on his face. "Anywhere—like the Greenfield Inn!"

Everyone seemed stunned by this announcement.

"The Greenfield Inn? The little hotel right here in town?" Karen said.

"How in the world do you know that?" Alan asked.

"It was the oddest thing," Raymond said. "Some of the other roadies I know—the ones who are here from out of town—are staying at that same hotel. Just before I came here, I gave an old buddy a ride back to the hotel, and that's when I saw him in the parking lot."

He pointed at the picture. "I'd seen him helping out yesterday and he'd seemed friendly enough, so I waved hello. But this time, he wasn't friendly at all."

"What did he do?" Violet wanted to know.

"He didn't wave back. He looked at me as if I were a ghost. And then he hurried back to his room," Raymond replied.

"He must know you're the Greenfield Four's roadie," said Alan.

"He does," said Jessie. "When we were looking for you yesterday, Raymond, he knew who you were."

"It sounds like he didn't want you to know he was at the Greenfield Inn," said Henry.

"When did this happen?" Alan asked.

"About an hour ago," Raymond answered.

"Oh, no," said Jessie. "He might not be there much longer. We need to hurry!"

* * * *

At the Greenfield Inn, darkness was beginning to fall, and crickets were chirping in the bushes. The Aldens and Raymond glanced around the parking lot, looking for the white van. There were several other cars and trucks parked in front of the rooms where people were staying, but no sign of the van.

"What do we do now?" Benny asked.

"We'll wait for Officer Weiss," Jessie reminded him. They had called him to tell him what they'd discovered about the man with the glasses and beret. Now, as they stood and waited behind Raymond's car, they wondered what would happen next.

"I think the thief is staying in Room 12," Raymond said, pointing to a door at the very end of the long motel building. "That's where he was going when I saw him earlier today."

A light was still on in the window of Room 12, but the shades had been pulled down.

Suddenly, the door opened, and Jon Emmott stepped out. He was still wearing his black beret, but he no longer had his glasses on. He looked around, but he didn't notice the children watching him from across the parking lot. He slung his bag over his shoulder and walked to the corner of the building, then turned and headed towards the back.

"Where's he going?" Violet whispered. Her heart was racing. *Was he going to get away?*

"Let's go see," Henry said.

"Yes, but let's try to keep our distance," Raymond said.

They followed Jon Emmott as he turned another corner and disappeared. They turned the corner, too, and at last they saw the white van with the blue stripe.

"He parked it where no one would see it," Jessie whispered.

They could see Jon Emmott grinning to himself as he started the van and waited for the engine to warm up. "Excuse me," Henry called out. "Aren't you Jon Emmott?"

The man's smile disappeared as quickly as it had come. "How do you know that?" he demanded.

Raymond spoke up. "That's not important right now," he said. "What's important is that you give back all those instruments you stole from the Greenfield Four."

"Forget it," Emmott said in a nasty voice. "Now get out of my way."

"I don't think you're going anywhere," said a voice behind the Aldens. The children turned around. It was Officer Weiss.

Jon Emmott turned off the engine of the van. His shoulders sagged, and he put his head down.

It was over.

CHAPTER 10

It's Not Over Till It's Over

At the police station, Jon Emmott confessed everything.

"I had to do it," he said. "I had to get even with them. I didn't want them to be so successful without me. Then, when I heard about the festival and the man from the record company, I wanted to ruin it for them."

"So you broke into their rehearsal studio," Henry said. "You guessed the security code."

Jon Emmott smiled bitterly. "You figured out I did that, didn't you? Yes, I was lucky that the new code wasn't very different from the old code.

"At first I wasn't going to sell the stolen instruments," Jon went on. "My only plan was to ruin the show."

"Well, you didn't ruin it," Jessie said. "They're still going to do their best and play tonight."

Jon's eyes narrowed. "I knew it wouldn't be enough to stop them." He chuckled.

The children looked at each other. They couldn't help but think there was something Jon Emmott wasn't telling them.

"Wait a minute," Henry spoke up. "What were you working on at the festival yesterday?"

Jon paused for a moment, then said stiffly, "I'm not sure what you're talking about."

"You were working on something while the stage was being built." Jessie insisted. "Something with wires and cables."

"Aren't you an electrician?" Violet asked.

"Come on, Jon," Raymond said sharply. "It's over. You'll just get yourself into more trouble if you don't tell us."

All eyes were on Jon. He looked at Officer Weiss. Finally he said, "I set up a timer under the stage so that the electricity would go off during the Greenfield Four's show."

The children looked at each other in disbelief.

"When is it supposed to go off?" Jessie asked.

"Eight-thirty," Jon replied. The Aldens checked their watches—that was less than an hour from now!

"Where did you put the timer?" Henry asked.

"In the back, by the right side of the stage," Jon told them.

"We'd better get over there," Violet said.

"And fast!" Benny added.

* * * *

By the time Raymond and the Aldens got to the festival, the Greenfield Four had just gone onstage. The children could see a man in the front row wearing a white suit and a wide hat. He didn't look happy, but he didn't look unhappy, either. He was paying close attention to the show.

"That must be the man from the record company," Violet said.

"We need to hurry," said Jessie. "That timer might go off any minute now!"

They rushed to the back of the stage. The crawl space underneath the stage was covered by a dark curtain. Henry flipped it up and peered underneath. Raymond had brought two flashlights and handed him one.

"Be very careful, Henry," Violet said. "Those wires and cables can be dangerous!"

"I wouldn't touch one if you gave me a million dollars," Henry told her, looking at the cables as if they were live snakes. "I just want to find the timer and stop it." He checked his watch. It read eight-twenty-five.

Henry and Raymond turned on their flashlights and crawled in. The noise coming from the stage above them was tremendous. Henry could feel the drums beating. They crawled around cardboard boxes, instrument cases, and packing crates. Henry and Raymond pointed their flashlights everywhere.

"Henry?" Raymond asked. "Did you find it?"

"No, not yet," Henry answered.

Then Henry pushed aside a large box and he saw glowing red numbers underneath.

The timer. And there were less than three minutes left!

"Here it is!" he called out. Raymond, on his hands and knees, crawled over as fast as he could.

The timer was a simple metal box. There were four small buttons, but they weren't marked. Henry watched as the red numbers counted down. *2:00...1:59...1:58...*

Henry reached out slowly and pushed the first button. Nothing happened. He pushed the second button, and nothing happened again. The timer kept going down— *1:33...1:32...1:31...*

He tried the third button.

Still nothing. *1:10...1:09...1:08...*

Henry's heart was pounding like mad now. Only one button left. He pressed it.

And then something happened.

"Uh-oh," Henry said.

The red numbers vanished for a moment. Then they reappeared. Now they said "0:10." Ten seconds!

Raymond saw this. "Jon set the timer up so it would go into a fast countdown if someone tried to shut it off!" he cried.

Henry didn't say anything. He just watched with a helpless feeling as the numbers counted down.

0:03...0:02...0:01...

Suddenly, there was a loud CLICK!

Everything went dark.

There was a loud gasp from the crowd. Suddenly, it was pitch black on the stage, and the entire festival was lit only by the glow of the full moon.

The members of the Greenfield Four turned around and looked at the three Alden children who were standing by the stage. For a moment they all stared at each other, frozen.

Then Violet had an idea.

"Play that new song of yours," she called to Karen, "with the acoustic guitars."

Benny wanted to asked what "acoustic" meant, but then he remembered—an acoustic instrument was one that didn't need any power in order to make sound.

"Good idea," Alan said with a nod.

Alan turned back to the crowd. "Well, it looks like someone forgot to pay the electric bill this month," he said. Everyone laughed. "So, until we can get the problem fixed, the band would like to play a nice little song that we wrote a few months ago with some instruments that don't need any electricity."

Dave came out from behind his drum set and tapped his sticks together. Amy and Karen picked up their acoustic guitars. Then Alan led the band down the steps at the side of the stage and onto the ground. They walked into the middle of the crowd, and the four of them began to play. Within minutes the audience was singing and clapping along to the beautiful song.

When they finished, the crowd gave them thunderous applause. Then, suddenly, all the lights came on, and the audience clapped again for Raymond and the rest of the crew who had fixed the electricity. A night that could have been a disaster had turned into something magical instead.

After the show, behind the stage, Alan Keller patted Henry on the back.

"You did it, my friend."

"Not fast enough," Henry said, frowning. Karen waved her hand to show that this was a silly idea. "We covered it up pretty well with that acoustic song."

"And that was Violet's brilliant idea," Amy pointed out. Violet blushed.

"That's my sister," Jessie said, putting her arm around her.

Then the man in the white walked towards them. It was the man who owned the record company.

"I have to tell you, I was very impressed by

the way you handled that power failure," he said. "It takes a band with a lot of smarts and experience to do that. You made sure to keep the crowd's attention. You knew exactly how to make sure the show went on."

"Thank you," Amy Keller replied.

"A band with that kind of talent is exactly the type of band I'd like to have making music for me," he told them, putting his hand out so Alan could shake it. "Congratulations, I'd like the Greenfield Four to record an album for me."

The members of the band were speech-less. Then, finally, Alan Keller said, "Well, we'd like to take all the credit for tonight's show, but we had a little help. In fact, we had a lot," he said, looking at the Aldens.

"Oh?"

"That's right," Karen continued. "These kids solve mysteries as well as we make music—maybe even better."

"I don't know that's true, " said Violet.

"Now, don't be modest," Alan replied. "If it weren't for the four of you, we would've sounded awful tonight." Alan quickly explained the whole story. "In fact, we've talked it over and decided to write a song about it. We'll call it 'The Ballad of the Aldens.'"

The children didn't know what to say, but the man from the record company did. "Sounds like your first big hit," he said.

"The first of many," Violet added.

Then Benny, dazzled by the thought of being mentioned in a song, said, "Wow, I'll be famous!"

Everyone laughed. "Too famous to go on solving mysteries?" Henry asked him.

Benny smiled. "No," he replied. "I'll never stop doing that. Ever!"